About the Author

Having spent most of my working life as a professional dance instructor, designing and producing theatrical shows for children, fantasy, fun and adventure are close to my heart. When a severe back injury resulting from a car crash forced me into early retirement, I started looking for new ways to be creative and enthuse children.

Inspiration came from my son, an underwater videographer and marine conservationist. Scuba diving with my son on Australia's Barrier Reef as part of my rehabilitation, revealed a magical world full of vibrant colours and incredible creatures. I began writing and *Reef Adventures* was born.

REEF
ADVENTURES
COLLECTION

Chloe Scarlett

REEF ADVENTURES COLLECTION

Nightingale Books

A CIP catalogue record for this title is
available from the British Library.

ISBN 9781838750 01-5

Nightingale Books is an imprint of
Pegasus Elliot MacKenzie Publishers Ltd.
www.pegasuspublishers.com

First Published in 2020

Nightingale Books
Sheraton House Castle Park
Cambridge England

Printed & Bound in Great Britain

Dedication

I would like to dedicate this book to the amazing people who tirelessly strive to clean and protect our oceans and their inhabitants. They give their time, effort and resources to ensure the continued existence of this marine world and for that I am grateful.

I hope that reading these stories will inspire children to grow up understanding the beauty and fragility of nature and help foster a desire to protect it.

Acknowledgements

Firstly, I want to thank my parents for introducing me, at an early age, to the magical and colourful world of theatre. When forced to leave this profession in later life, I tentatively stepped into another magical and colourful domain, the world of writing.

An enormous and heartfelt thank you to some very special and wonderful people I am lucky enough to have in my life.

My sons, Richard, Adam and Sam.
My brother, Clive.
My friends, Jeannette and Wendy.
My granddaughter, Lucy, for her suggestions and telling me if my stories were any good!
My incredibly talented and very patient illustrator, Elisabeth Gerlitz.

These people believed in me from the start and have continued to give me their unflinching support during this journey.

Finally, a special thank you to Adam, without whom *Reef Adventures* would not have happened. His phenomenal knowledge and expertise of the underwater world has ensured that my stories and their characters are authentic. He has spent many hours, writing letters and sending submissions to agents, in an attempt to get me published. Even when I wanted to give up, he wouldn't, and here we are today. His hard work has paid off and *Reef Adventures* is now a reality.

Thank you to you all and to your families for helping me to make a dream come true.

Contents

THE MERMAID'S MASK

Did you know, that the world is shaped like a gigantic round ball and that it consists of two halves called hemispheres, the Northern Hemisphere and the Southern Hemisphere?

In the Southern Hemisphere, is a country called Australia, which you may have heard of? Australia is a vast country, with lots of different types of scenery. There are huge areas of sandy desert, lots of flat plains and grasslands, rugged mountains and cliffs and also beautiful beaches, perfect for playing in the sea and building sandcastles.

Australia is divided into six parts called states, and this story is set along the coast of a state called Queensland, in the north-east of Australia. Along this coastline is an area called The Great Barrier Reef, set in the Coral Sea and stretching more than 2,300 kilometres, making it the largest reef in the world.

This may be hard to believe, but the Great Barrier Reef is about the size of seventy million football pitches, and astronauts can see it from the moon!

Over 1,500 different kinds of fish live in the Great Barrier Reef, and as you read these stories, you will get to know some of these. The smallest fish is the stout infantfish, which is only about seven millimetres long and the biggest, is the whale shark, which can grow up to twelve metres long!

The Great Barrier Reef is very beautiful, consisting of many different types of brightly coloured coral. The sun is scorching here and so high that, if you imagine yourself being under the sea, the sun will shine through the water, making everything very clear and bright, rather like a gigantic underwater rainbow!

Within this magical underwater world, coral grows in many shapes and colours. Coral provides both food and shelter for countless sea creatures you will meet in these stories. Now that you can picture where this story is set, let's get on with it, shall we?

"Hello children, my name is Grandpa Terence, and I'm one of the largest and oldest turtles, living on the Great Barrier Reef. I have two little grandchildren called Tillie Turtle and Tommie Turtle, who are twins and today they have come to visit me. Tillie and Tommie love to hear my stories about my life, and we are just about to begin one, so you might like to hear it, too."

Grandpa Terence looked at Tommie and smiled. "Stop fidgeting Tommie and sit still."

"I'm excited Grandpa," replied Tommie, "I so love your stories."

"Today's story is called *The Mermaid's Mask*," said Grandpa Terence.

"Have you seen a mermaid then Grandpa?" asked Tillie excitedly.

"I've seen many mermaids," replied Grandpa Terence.

"But that can't be true, Grandpa, mermaids aren't real, are they?" questioned Tommie.

"Well, it's up to you what you choose to believe," replied Grandpa Terence, "but I know what I've seen, so listen to my story, and then you can decide for yourselves."

"I was about sixteen years old," began Grandpa Terence, "I belonged to the Turtle Scout Brigade and one evening at the end of one of our meetings, we were told some very exciting news. The Turtle Scouts had been asked to provide a Guard of Honour, at a Grand Ball, being given by the Mer King and Queen, where their son, Prince Philander, was to choose his new mermaid bride."

"You must have been so thrilled, Grandpa!" squealed Tillie.

"I certainly was, but that wasn't all," replied Grandpa Terence. "Not only was I to be part of the Guard of Honour, but I was chosen to escort the Prince and his new Princess, back to the Mer Palace, after the Ball."

"Wow!" exclaimed Tommie, "what an honour for you Grandpa."

"Indeed, it was, but now, let's get on with the story, shall we? For many weeks leading up to the Grand Ball, preparations were taking place, and by the time the actual day arrived, my scout friends and I were about ready to burst with excitement. However, I also felt a little nervous about the huge responsibility I had been given.

"The Ball was taking place in the Great Cave. To enter the Great Cave, you had to swim through a tunnel in an Orange Coral Mountain, and this tunnel opened up into a vast cave. The top of the cave," explained Grandpa Terence, "was completely open, which allowed the sunlight to shine down, causing beautiful reflections on the large pool of water, which filled the cave.

"When my friends and I arrived at the cave, on the day of the Ball, our eyes opened wide in wonder, and our jaws dropped in utter amazement. The walls of the cave had been completely covered in coloured lights, which reflected on the water like a gigantic rainbow.

"On one side of the pool two glimmering golden thrones had been erected for the Mer King and Queen and, on either side of these, stood two, slightly smaller thrones made in exquisite shiny pearls, which we thought must be for Prince Philander and his new Princess.

"Around the edges of the pool, the rock formations had been flattened and, in their place, now stood many small coral seats for the guests. There were also tables filled with the most incredible assortment of food, for the Royal Banquet.

"I stared at this magical sight for quite a while, until I was brought back to earth by my scout leader's voice, telling us that we needed to get prepared, as the Mer Royal Family were due to arrive at any moment.

"My scout friends and I formed two lines down either side of the entrance tunnel, which was now glowing with bright lights and waited with anticipation for the Mer Royal Family to arrive.

"Suddenly a trumpeter started playing a fanfare, and we all stood to attention as the Royal Party came into view. Two turtles, one carrying the Mer King and Queen and one carrying Prince Philander, entered the tunnel and, as they passed by, we all saluted.

"The two turtles looked so proud as they brought their distinguished guests into the cave and I suddenly felt very nervous that I was to perform the same task at the end of the evening, for the return to the Mer Palace. My mind started spinning as I tried to remember the instructions I had been given. You must swim very smoothly and slowly, no sudden jolts or turns; that would cause discomfort to my precious cargo.

"I was jerked back into the moment when my friend Tarquin said:

"'Come on, Terence, stop daydreaming, time for us to join in the fun.'

"As we took our places in one corner of the pool, a royal attendant positioned himself at the tunnel entrance, ready to announce the arrival of the Mer Princesses, all hoping to become the new Royal Bride.

"'Princess Persephone!' he announced, as the most beautiful mermaid appeared from the tunnel. She had a shiny pink tail, her hair was the same colour pink and, hiding her face, was an exquisite pink glittery mask.

"'Princess Ariadne!' continued the attendant, and in came the next princess, with emerald-green hair and tail and again her face was covered with a mask, this time in emerald-green jewels.

"One by one the beautiful princesses arrived, their hair, tails and masks, all matching in vivid colours; reds, yellows, turquoises, purples, oranges, blues and much more.

"Finally, the last princess was announced, and just when I thought that she couldn't possibly be any more beautiful than those who had gone before her, I gasped in amazement as I was proven wrong.

"Princess Pearl entered, and all the guests gasped in awe as they saw her. Her hair and tail were shimmering in the brightest silver I had ever seen, she wore a silver and pearl necklace and bracelets, and her silver mask was glinting so brightly, that I had to squint my eyes to look at it.

"As the last princess appeared, all the guests cheered and the party was in full swing.

"'Why are they all wearing masks?' I asked my scout leader.

"'Well, it is so the prince can't see their faces and therefore choose his future wife on her beauty alone. His parents insist that his bride should also have inner beauty and show that she is kind and caring within. They say that if the Prince finds the most gentle and sweet princess, then, in his eyes, she will also be the most beautiful to look at.'

"I thought these words sounded very wise, but didn't understand how this was going to come about.

"'The prince will dance and speak to all of the princesses in turn and must make his choice before they remove their masks,' continued my scout leader.

"He was right. As the evening progressed, the prince did indeed dance with each princess in turn. As the Ball drew to its end, we were all asked to be silent as the announcement was made about the chosen princess.

"Suddenly, the silence was broken as a poor seal waiter, carrying a tray of glasses, slipped on some liquid from a spilt drink and, as he fell to the floor, the glasses broke with a loud shattering crash.

"I was amazed at what happened next. I heard one of the Princesses say:

"'What a clumsy fool, he looks so ridiculous!'

"'Yes,' replied the Princess next to her, 'but after all, he's only an unimportant waiter, with no grace or social skills, he should be sacked!'

"I was horrified to discover that such cruel words could come from the mouths of such beautiful creatures, and I immediately understood what my scout leader was talking about, when he said beauty comes from within and don't be fooled by appearances.

"Then, before our eyes, something wonderful happened. The Silver Mermaid moved over to where the embarrassed waiter stood and put her arms around him, she said, in a very gentle voice:

"'Oh, dear, accidents do happen, don't they, please let me help you up.'

"The seal waiter gratefully took her arm, and as he then started to pick up the broken glass, the Silver Mermaid helped him.

"'There, that didn't take long,' she said, 'I'm so glad you're not hurt.'

The guests all looked on in stunned silence, but I noticed that the Mer King, Queen and the prince were whispering together as they watched the scene unfold.

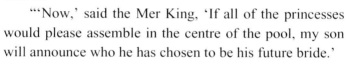

"'Now,' said the Mer King, 'If all of the princesses would please assemble in the centre of the pool, my son will announce who he has chosen to be his future bride.'

"The princesses did as requested, and Prince Philander stood between his parents, ready to announce his decision.

"'Ladies and gentleman, this has been an enjoyable evening, and I thank you and all of these lovely princesses for coming along. I was almost sure who I was going to choose as the night came to its end, and then something happened which confirmed my decision as being right. One of these mermaids displayed kindness and compassion beyond compare, towards one of my staff, something I had already felt she had when I spoke with her earlier. My chosen mermaid is Princess Pearl!'

"Prince Philander then came forward and removed Princess Pearl's mask, and the most beautiful face was revealed to all. As Prince Philander took Princess Pearl's hand, he tossed the mask into the pool, and everyone clapped and cheered.

"I knew that this was my cue to move towards them, ready to take them to the Mer Palace. Decorated seats had already been strapped to my back, and as the Prince and Princess sat in these, I was cautious to be still, so as not to knock them off balance.

"The trumpeter then sounded another fanfare, and I very steadily began the short journey to the Palace, amidst cheers and cries of joy from all the guests, who were delighted with the Prince's choice of bride.

"As we reached the Palace forecourt, I stopped very gently and waited for the royal couple to climb down from my shell. Princess Pearl came and stroked my head and thanked me for a perfect ride.

"Prince Philander turned to me and said it was the best ride he had ever had and would I like to be his and Princess Pearl's driver, as he felt he could trust me with the Princess's safety.

"I was astonished by this incredible offer and graciously accepted.

"As I made my way back home, I was singing to myself with sheer joy at my new position and that, Tillie and Tommie, became my life's work.

"Everywhere Prince Philander and Princess Pearl went, I took them. They were always very kind to me, and I thoroughly enjoyed working for them. When I eventually retired from my job, I was presented with a beautiful crest on which was engraved: To Dear Terence, for your caring support, hard work and loyalty. Our very best wishes, King Philander and Queen Pearl. By now, they had come to the throne and were the new rulers of the Mer Kingdom.

"Oh Grandpa," said Tilly, "I think that is my favourite of all your stories, I loved it."

"Me too," added Tommie. "Grandpa, could you take us to see The Great Cave, where the story took place?"

"I'm not sure," replied Grandpa Terence, "it happened such a long time ago, I don't even know whether it's possible to get into the cave, now."

"PLEASE Grandpa, can we try?" continued Tommie.

"Please, please, PLEASE," joined in Tillie.

"Very well," said Grandpa, "I will try to okay it with your mummy and daddy, and if they agree, I will take you next Sunday."

The following Sunday morning, Tommie and Tillie were bouncing up and down with excitement, as they waited for Grandpa Terence to arrive.

As they waved goodbye to their parents and followed Grandpa Terence, they both felt as if they were going on a fabulous adventure.

It was quite a long swim to the Orange Coral Mountain, where the Great Cave was, and Tommie and Tillie were beginning to feel a bit tired, but they didn't dare tell Grandpa Terence, in case he decided to turn back home. Eventually, Orange Coral Mountain appeared in the distance, and the young turtles' tiredness instantly vanished and was replaced by uncontrollable excitement. As they reached the Coral Mountain, the cave entrance was still there and looked accessible.

"Now, you two," said Grandpa Terence, "you will wait here while I go in and check that we can get into the cave, and it is safe. Do not move from this spot until I return," he commanded.

Tommie and Tillie nodded their acceptance of his instruction, knowing that if they disobeyed, Grandpa wouldn't let them go any further.

They waited patiently for a few minutes and then Grandpa Terence returned to them. "It's amazing," he cried, "just as I remembered it from all those years ago. There are no marine animals of course and no lights or decorations, but I can still picture it just as it was then and, hopefully, you will be able to imagine what it was like. Come along then, children, follow me, very carefully."

The twins followed Grandpa Terence into the tunnel, staying very close to him because it was dark and then, as it seemed to become light ahead of them, they suddenly found themselves in the Great Cave. The children gasped in amazement, as the cave was enormous.

"Now," said Grandpa Terence, "partly close your eyes and 'see' all those sparkling lights, glimmering around the cave. Look at the sun beating down onto the water. Listen; can you hear the band playing? Look at all the beautiful princesses and look, over there, the Mer King and Queen seated on their thrones, watching Prince Philander and Princess Pearl dancing together."

"Oh yes, Grandpa, I can see it!" squealed Tillie.

"I love the music, it makes me want to dance too!" exclaimed Tommie.

They stayed there for quite a time, enjoying the experience. Grandpa Terence was reliving wonderful memories of long ago and Tommie and Tillie let their imaginations transport them into a magical scene that their grandfather had explained so well.

After a while, Grandpa Terence broke the silence, "I'm afraid it's time for us to head back home now," he said.

"Okay, Grandpa," replied Tillie obediently, and Tommie said, "Thank you so much, Grandpa, for bringing us here."

As they started to swim back towards the tunnel entrance, Tillie suddenly cried, "Grandpa, what's that down there, something shiny behind that piece of coral?"

Grandpa Terence swam down to look behind the coral and what he retrieved was unbelievable, "A SILVER MASK!"

"Oh, my goodness," he said. "I wonder if this could be…?

"Princess Pearl's!" the twins cried together.

"It's still so shiny," said Tillie.

"That's because it never lost its magic," replied Grandpa.

"Can I keep it, Grandpa?" asked Tillie.

"I don't think so," replied Grandpa Terence, "I think its secret should remain in this magical place."

Tommie and Tillie reluctantly agreed as Grandpa Terence hid the mask back behind the coral.

They made their way back through the tunnel, and just as they came out of the other end, there was a loud roaring sound behind them. They turned to see the tunnel collapsing, making it impossible for anyone ever to gain access again. When the roaring sound of falling rock had stopped, Grandpa Terence turned to Tommie and Tillie, hiding behind him for safety and said:

"I think that you are fortunate children, you were meant to see this secret place and feel its magic, and now that you have done that, it is hidden forever and all its secrets, too."

As they made their way back home, desperate to tell their parents about their beautiful day, Tommie and Tillie sang, "We believe in Mermaids, we believe in mermaids."

"Grandpa," asked Tillie, "do you think Mummy and Daddy will believe our story too?"

"I have a feeling they will," replied Grandpa Terence, "I'm sure they will remember how it feels from their childhoods and will want to experience the magic and excitement, with you. Come along, not far now until we're safely back home."

So, you see, children, it's always important, never to judge anyone by the way they look, even if they are different to you. It's the type of person they are inside that matters.

Remember to believe in your dreams and let your imagination run wild. Whether your beliefs turn out to be right or wrong, doesn't matter, what does matter, is that you will always hold onto the magic of those beliefs and in time, pass them on to your children and grandchildren, just like Grandpa Terence.

Do YOU believe in Mermaids?

THE DAY AT THE DENTIST

"Come along, children, hurry up, we must not be late," Mrs Shark called to her children. She turned to Mr Shark and asked, "Are you ready my dear?"

"I don't want to go and see a dentist," he replied. "You know I don't like them."

"Why are you so nervous?" questioned Mrs Shark.

"Because I'm scared Selena, always have been," confessed her husband.

"Now come along Socrates, there is no need to be nervous, the dentist is not going to hurt you. Anyway, you don't have a choice; you've been suffering from a toothache for a while now, and it won't heal itself."

Just then Saskia and Simon, Mr and Mrs Shark's children, came into the room.

"What's the matter with Daddy?" asked Simon. "He looks pale."

"Daddy doesn't want to go to the dentist, he is feeling very nervous," his mother replied.

"You silly Daddy," continued Saskia. "You're big and strong and not afraid of anything!"

"I'm afraid my darlings that being big and strong has nothing to do with it. I am scared, and that's all there is to it."

"If you're brave the dentist will give you a sticker Daddy," said Simon.

Before allowing her husband to reply as to his feelings about being given a sticker, she interrupted and said, "Come on everyone, let's go. Oh, by the way, our usual dentist Mr Drill has retired, so we are seeing his replacement today. He is a surgeonfish called Mr Surgeon, and I have heard many excellent reports about him."

"Ha, ha, ha," laughed Simon, "Mr Surgeon, the dental surgeon, how funny is that?"

Saskia started to laugh as well, but all Mr Shark said was, "Well that's just great. Not only do I have to see a dentist, but I have to see the new kid on the block as well!"

"Don't be so grumpy!" said Selina, "Pull yourself together and set an example for the children. They are not scared of the dentist, and we don't want them to be!"

While Saskia and Simon skipped and played on the journey to the dentist, Mr Shark remained silent. On the way, they met Mr and Mrs Goby and their daughter Gabrielle, who went to school with Saskia and Simon. The parents exchanged greetings, and while they chatted,

Saskia, Simon and Gabrielle played chase the tail. Suddenly, Mrs Goby said, "We have just been to see the new dentist, he is very charming and efficient."

"Ooooh," groaned Mr Shark as his wife told Mrs Goby that was where they were heading to now.

"You don't seem too keen, Socrates," said Mr Goby.

"Rather be anywhere else," came Socrates' reply.

"It has been quite a while since we had a catch-up, would you all like to join us for tea this afternoon?"

"Can we Mummy, please?" asked Saskia.

"That would be delightful, thank you very much," replied Mrs Shark.

The children cheered happily as Mrs Goby said: "Would five o'clock be convenient for you?"

"Perfect, and thank you," replied Mrs Shark.

They all said their goodbyes and went on their way. Everyone was looking forward to going out for tea, except Mr Shark, who groaned, "That's great, I've got a sore tooth, and we go out for tea. Lots of lovely food and I won't be able to eat it."

"You are in a bad mood today, Socrates," said his wife. "I'm telling you, if you let the dentist sort your tooth, then I'm sure you will be able to eat tea and enjoy yourself with everyone else."

As they entered the dental surgery, Miss Ramona, the dentist receptionist, greeted them. "Good morning, Shark family," she said brightly, "Mr Surgeon will see you shortly."

No sooner had she spoken than Mr Surgeon appeared. "Good morning everyone, I am Mr Surgeon your new dentist."

"Good morning, we are very pleased to meet you," replied Mrs Shark, "This is my husband Socrates, my children Saskia and Simon and I am Selena."

"Now, who is going to be the first lucky shark to try out my new chair?" asked Mr Surgeon.

"Me, Me, Me!" the children exclaimed together, while their father looked on in amazement at their enthusiasm.

"I think, ladies first," replied Mr Surgeon. "Come along, Selena, in you come."

Mr Surgeon happily informed Mrs Shark her teeth were in excellent condition and needed no attention. However, before she went out of the surgery, she asked Mr Surgeon if she could have a little chat with him about her husband.

As they joined the rest of the family, Mr Surgeon and Mrs Shark had big smiles on their faces, but they didn't tell anyone why.

"Come along Saskia, you're next," said Mr Surgeon and Saskia followed him into the surgery and jumped up into his new chair. "How about a little ride first?" said Mr Surgeon.

"Yes please," replied Saskia excitedly. Mr Surgeon then pressed the controls to make the chair go up and down and turn around. Saskia giggled as she enjoyed the ride. "Now, time for business," said Mr Surgeon, "Open wide, Saskia and let me see how your beautiful teeth are doing.

"No problems there," continued Mr Surgeon, "You just need to brush a little more thoroughly behind your teeth, it's easy to forget to do that, so try a little harder please."

"I will, Mr Surgeon," replied Saskia and as she came out of the room she said excitedly to her brother, "Simon, the chair ride is amazing, and I've got two stickers!"

"My turn now!" exclaimed Simon and he followed Mr Surgeon into his room. Simon also loved the chair ride, but when Mr Surgeon examined his teeth, he told Simon that he would need a little filling.

"That's okay," replied Simon and Mr Surgeon went out to inform Mr and Mrs Shark about Simon's filling.

"That's fine, please go ahead," said Mrs Shark.

As Mr Surgeon went back into his room, Mr Shark gasped and said, "What is he going to do to Simon, will he hurt him?"

"No, no, dear, not at all," replied his wife. "Mr Surgeon will freeze Simon's gum and then fill the small hole in his tooth with a unique material, very straightforward."

Mr Shark groaned loudly and again looked very pale.

Simon soon reappeared with a big smile on his face and waving two stickers in his fin. "You're right sis, that chair ride is awesome, when can we come again, Mr Surgeon?"

"I think in six months' time will be okay," he replied with a smile on his face.

"Your turn now, Daddy," said Saskia.

"Be brave Daddy, and you might get two stickers," chuckled Simon rather naughtily.

"You two, please sit here quietly and read a comic while I go in with Daddy," said Mrs Shark. "Miss Ramona will be watching you."

Once inside the surgery Mr Shark became frozen to the spot. "I can't do this; I'm just so scared!"

"Now Socrates, I understand," said Mr Surgeon, "we will take things very slowly. I want you to breathe deeply and try to relax, all I'm going to do is just look at your teeth. I won't do anything without telling you first."

With Selena's encouragement, Socrates finally managed to sit in the dentist's large adult chair, and as he did so, he exclaimed, "Before you ask — NO, I don't want a chair ride thank you!"

As Mr Surgeon tried not to smile, Socrates very slowly opened his big shark mouth. Suddenly, he closed it again in amazement as Mr Surgeon swam away from him and exclaimed, "I CAN'T DO IT, I CAN'T, I'M JUST TOO SCARED!"

"What?" said Socrates as Selena did her best to hide the smile that was creeping across her face.

"What do you mean, Mr Surgeon, you can't be scared, you're the dentist. I'm the one who should be afraid, the patient!"

Mr Surgeon then gave Selina a sly wink and said, "Tell you what we'll do Socrates, man to man, you tell me what you're scared of, and I'll tell you what I'm afraid of, do we have a deal?"

"All right, just between you and me, our secret," replied Socrates.

"Perhaps you would like to wait outside please Selena, we'll be okay here." requested Mr Surgeon.

As Selena left the room it was all she could do to stop herself from laughing; it seemed as if the little plan she and Mr Surgeon had devised was going to work.

"Where's Daddy?" asked Saskia.

"He'll be out shortly, he's okay," replied their mother.

The children didn't understand what was going on but decided not to press their mother, as she was now reading a magazine, which suggested, 'Conversation over, no more questions.'

Back in the surgery, Mr Surgeon and Socrates were confiding in each other.

"I think I may have had an unusually bad experience as a child when I visited the dentist." began Socrates. "All I know is that it's left me with this fear of pain."

"Well," began Mr Surgeon, "Things have moved a long way since you were a child and I can honestly say that, if you let me look at and possibly treat your teeth, the most you may experience is a little discomfort, certainly not pain."

"Wow, that's some promise, I think I believe you, though," Socrates replied. "However, you said you were too scared to look in my mouth, why is that?"

"Because Socrates, you are a shark, I'm afraid you might swallow me!"

"Ha, ha, ha, ha, ha!" laughed Socrates loudly. "Are you serious? Of course, I won't eat you; I wouldn't get my teeth fixed then, would I?"

As they both dissolved into fits of laughter, Selina on hearing them couldn't help but join in.

"Why is everyone laughing, Mummy?" asked Simon.

Through her chuckles, Selena told the children that she would let Daddy explain later.

As he allowed Mr Surgeon to swim around the inside of his mouth, examining his teeth, Socrates finally felt at ease.

"Well," said Mr Surgeon finally, "Your teeth are in good condition Socrates, but I'm afraid the one causing you the trouble will have to come out." Before Socrates had a chance to object, Mr Surgeon continued. "Don't panic, I will explain the whole procedure to you. Firstly, I am going to spray your gum to numb it a little and then I will give you an injection in your gum. You will only feel a slight prick Socrates, and I'm sure you can handle that."

Once Socrates' gum was frozen, and he couldn't feel, anything, Mr Surgeon proceeded to attach a particular piece of wire around Socrates' tooth. This was connected to a winch-type instrument, which was only used to remove shark teeth, as they were so big. Mr Surgeon then proceeded to press the button and, as the winch began to turn, *Whoosh*, out popped Socrates' tooth.

"All done," said Mr Surgeon.

"But I didn't feel a thing, that's incredible!" replied Socrates.

"I kept my promise, and you kept yours," said Mr Surgeon and they both dissolved again into fits of laughter.

Once he had composed himself, Mr Surgeon said, "You may need to take a couple of painkillers when the numbness wears off, as it may be a little uncomfortable for a short while, but the discomfort shouldn't last long."

As they rejoined the rest of the family, Mrs Shark and the children were anxious to know how their father had got on. "Little difficult to speak until the numbness wears off," replied their father, "But I really don't understand what fish make all the fuss about. Dentist, nothing to it, a piece of cake."

As the children listened in amazement, their father continued, "Talking of cake, we have a tea to get to, don't we? I'll just eat on the other side, for now, can't miss cake!"

The children laughed as they left the dentist surgery and they couldn't wait to hear why their father had such a change of heart.

"Right," said Selina, "I think some fun time in the park is in order, don't you?" The children agreed happily as their mother continued, "We must then pop to the supermarket for some groceries, and I think some of Daddy's favourite biscuits, he deserves them!"

Later that afternoon, the Shark family set out to visit their friends the Goby Family. As they entered the house, Mrs Goby asked how their visit to the dentist had gone.

"Very well, we found Mr Surgeon most polite and competent."

"What about you, Socrates?" laughed Mr Goby, "Don't tell me you allowed him to come near you?"

"Of course, no problem at all," replied Socrates. "Well, actually," he continued, "That's not exactly correct," I have an amusing story to tell you while we have tea."

As the friends took their places at the table, Socrates suddenly waved his fin in the air and said, "Guess what everyone, I'VE GOT TWO STICKERS AS WELL!!"

So you see children, it is very important to care for your teeth and clean them thoroughly and remember, as you've learnt from our story, there is no need to be afraid to visit the dentist.

HAPPY BRUSHING!

THE CRUSTACEAN CUP DERBY

There was much excitement on the Reef, as the day was fast approaching when the Crustacean Cup Derby took place. This day was a highlight of the year for the inhabitants of the Reef.

Many races took place, while stalls providing refreshments and fun and games appeared in abundance. Some of the games you may have seen and tried yourselves; such as hoopla, hook the duck (only the Reef game was called 'hook the octopus') and lucky dip.

There was a roundabout and helter-skelter and also a tug of war, where two teams of giant creatures held onto a very long piece of seaweed and tried to pull each other over a line in the seabed.

The final and most important event, was the Crustacean Cup Derby when crustaceans rode in chariots made from differently sized seashells. Talented seahorse jockeys pulled these magnificent chariots along.

A crustacean is a water creature, which has a protective shell covering its body, such as crabs, shrimps, and lobsters. Did you know that lobsters are orange, blue, white or yellow, but never red? They only turn red when they are cooked!

In the weeks leading up to this grand event, the competitors spent much of their time building and perfecting their chariots.

On the day of the derby, all competitors' names were entered into a draw, to decide which jockey was to pull each chariot. All the contestants' friends rallied round to help build the chariots, and on the day before the Derby, everyone was very busy with preparations.

Chico and Christopher who were crabs were busy helping their friend Calvin crab to tie the wheels onto his chariot. Binding them with seaweed did this. Many of the girls, including Clemmie a clownfish, Bella a butterflyfish and their friend Debbie a damselfish, carried out the task of seaweed searching for all the competitors.

Lawrence, Lenny and Lance the lionfish, were attaching the seat to the chariot of Salvador, their shrimp friend, while Leighton lobster was attaching his harness, with the help of fellow lobsters, Leopold and Lorenzo.

The big day finally arrived, and the atmosphere was filled with excitement. Squeals of laughter rang out as the fish children rode on the roundabout and hurtled down the helter-skelter. All enjoyed delicious refreshments as they joined in the fun of the day.

"It is now time for the children's races," a voice boomed out over the loudspeaker. The task of making the announcements had been given to Grandpa Terence, who was the Reef's current mayor. He took the job very seriously and his grandchildren, Tillie and Tommie, who you may remember, felt very proud as they heard his voice echoing across the crowds.

"The judging panel for the races consisted of Sebastian shrimp, Lysander lobster and Cuthbert crab," announced Grandpa Terence. "Shrimps one hundred metre sprint competitors, to the line please," Grandpa Terence continued. "Competitors entered are, girls; Shauna, Shanelle, Shanie and Shakaya and the boys; Silas, Stevie, Sinbad and Sammy."

The little shrimps lined up and waited for the gun to fire, to start the race. "Take your marks, get set, BANG!"

They all swam as fast as they could towards the finishing line, with crowds of parents and friends cheering them on. "The winner is SAMMY!" Everyone cheered as Sammy went to the judging table to collect his medal.

"Next, we have the young lobster three-legged race. Take your places with your partners please."

The young lobsters lined up, with one of their claws tied to their partners. There was Latisha with Leona, Loretta with Lucinda, Lloyd with Leander and Louis with Lathan.

"Take your marks, get set BANG!"

"Come on, faster!" everyone cheered encouragingly, as the young lobsters stumbled to the finish.

Then rang out Grandpa Terence's voice, "Well done everyone, that was very exciting, and the winners are LORETTA and LUCINDA!" The girls collected their medals with pride as the competitors for the final children's race lined up.

"Finally, we have the young crab's sack race, which I'm sure we will all find amusing!" continued Grandpa

Terence. "Competitors entered are girls; Crystal, Crissy and Cressida and boys; Cornelious, Cameron and Casper."

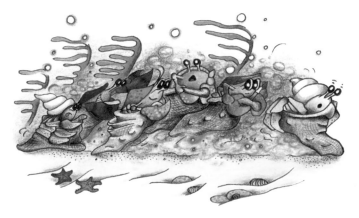

"Take your marks, get set, BANG!" How everyone cheered and laughed as the young crabs tried to bounce to the finish in their sacks.

"The winner is — oh, we have a tie," said Grandpa Terence. "The winners are, Crissy and Cameron!" As the children collected their medals, Grandpa Terence made the most important announcement of the day.

"Ladies, gentlemen and children, I will now announce the draw for the Derby competitors' drivers."

The crowd became silent, and everyone listened intently as the seahorses' names were announced and which driver they were assigned to with their chariots.

"Seahorse Hadley will pull for Salvador the shrimp. Seahorse Hamish will pull for Crispin, the crab. Seahorse Horace will pull for Leighton, the lobster. Seahorse Hayden will pull for Stavros, the shrimp. Seahorse

Hadrian will pull for Calvin, the crab. Seahorse Hercules will pull for Leo, the lobster."

Everyone cheered as the jockeys put on their competitors' colours and the chariots were lined up on the starting line. The drivers strapped themselves into their harnesses, and the crowd waited in anticipation with the drivers, for the race to start.

Suddenly the silence was broken by Grandpa Terence's voice.

"It is now my pleasure to announce the commencement of the biggest race of the day and the most important event of the Reef year. It is time for the Crustacean Cup Derby!"

Everyone was poised tensely and then, "Take your marks, and get set BANG!"

They were off, the noise from the spectators was incredible as the charioteers gripped onto their reins, desperately trying to steer their seahorse and chariot towards the finish line.

Suddenly, there was a loud crash! The cheers turned to gasps as the wheel fell off Calvin crab's chariot and he collided with Stavros shrimp. In no time at all, there was a big pile-up as the chariots ran into each other.

A stunned silence fell over everyone, which was quickly broken by Grandpa Terence. "Is anyone hurt? Paramedics to the scene please." Pedro and Percy the appointed parrotfish paramedics, immediately rushed forward to offer help.

Fortunately, nobody was seriously hurt, and everyone rallied round to help recover the chariots, most of which, miraculously suffered little damage. Poor Calvin crab was so relieved that Hadrian his seahorse was unhurt, but confused as to why the wheel had fallen off his chariot.

"There will be a thirty-minute delay while the competitors reassemble and we establish what happened," announced Grandpa Terence. "We will then hope to start the Derby again."

As Calvin was examining his broken chariot, he called his crab friends Christopher and Chico to help him. "I just don't understand it," said Calvin, "I strapped the wheel on myself and then while Christopher and I went to get my harness, you checked it for me, didn't you Chico?"

"Uhm, I... I... yes... I did," replied Chico, turning a beetroot-red colour. as he answered.

"What is it?" questioned Calvin. "Why are you looking so embarrassed?"

With that, Chico suddenly burst into tears. "I'm so sorry, I do not know what came over me," sobbed Chico.

"Stop snivelling and tell me what happened!" commanded Calvin.

Chico went on to explain that as Calvin had won the Derby for the last two years, he desperately wanted his brother Crispin to win. Crispin didn't know that when Chico was supposed to be checking Calvin's wheel, he had in fact loosened it, in the hope that it would slow Calvin down.

"I never meant for it to fall off," sobbed Chico, "I just wanted to slow you down and give Crispin a chance."

"YOU DID WHAT? THAT'S CHEATING!" screamed Calvin.

"How could you?" continued Christopher. "I thought you were Calvin's friend."

"I am, I am, it was just a stupid moment of madness, and I'm so very sorry Calvin, I never meant to hurt anyone. Please, please forgive me and still be my friend, Calvin."

Calvin was silent for a couple of minutes, and then he turned to Chico and said:

"I am so surprised that you could have considered doing such an unkind and foolish, let alone highly dangerous thing. However, I accept that you didn't intend to cause hurt or damage and I suppose we all act stupidly at times, including Christopher and myself. I'm very hurt by what you did to me, Chico, but I will accept your apology and will remain your friend, providing you accept the following conditions."

"Of course," replied Chico.

"You will help Christopher and I repair my chariot, and then you will confess your actions to the judging panel and accept whatever punishment they give you."

Chico agreed to Calvin's conditions without question, and as soon as the chariot was repaired, he went and confessed his actions to the judges, who were very angry. Lysander lobster almost, but not quite, turned red, as he shouted at Chico, telling him what a stupid, thoughtless and dangerous thing he had done. Cuthbert crab asked Chico to confirm that his brother, Crispin, wasn't aware of what Chico had done.

On receiving this confirmation, Sebastian shrimp declared that Crispin would therefore not be disqualified from the Derby re-run. He then went on to tell Chico; "Cheating is never acceptable. If you win by cheating, you are never the real winner. Life is about taking part and doing your best always, that is what is important and will give you self-worth and pride in your achievements. If you do happen to win at anything, you can then be extra proud, knowing that you became the winner fairly and squarely."

Chico was silent and felt very sheepish as he listened to the judges' lecture. He knew that they were right and that he thoroughly deserved the punishment they were going to give him.

Lysander lobster began, "My punishment will be, that after the race you will clean every competitors chariot, until it is gleaming!"

Cuthbert crab continued, "My punishment will be that you will wash all the jockeys' colours and make sure they are pristine and stored carefully for next year!"

Finally, Sebastian shrimp concluded, "My punishment will be, that tomorrow morning you will report early and help the stallholders to dismantle their booths and stow away their goods! You may think we are very hard on you, young Chico, but you must be made to understand and pay for your cruel and dangerous actions."

"Do you have anything to say for yourself?" questioned Lysander lobster.

"Just that I am so very sorry, and I will never be so unkind or cheat again," replied Chico.

"Very good, you may now go and watch the Derby," said Sebastian shrimp.

Chico breathed a sigh of relief as he made his way to the starting line. His punishments were hard, but he knew no more than he deserved. He went to wish his brother Crispin good luck and then went to tell Calvin and Christopher that he had been given his punishments. He apologised again and then wished his friend Calvin luck for the race. Calvin gave Chico a hug and then poised himself for the start.

"Take your marks, get set, BANG!" They were off, and as the chariots sped forward the crowd erupted into shouts and cheers, the false start from earlier forgotten.

As the chariots screeched around the halfway point, marked by a large purple shell, Calvin was in the lead just ahead of Crispin, Chico's brother.

"Come on Crispin! Faster Calvin!" came the cries of encouragement. As the two drivers approached the line neck and neck, it was impossible to know who was going to win. The seahorses reached forward with a final thrust, Crispin's chariot went over the line first.

"Hooray, congratulations!" were the cries from the crowd as Calvin stepped down from his chariot, patted his seahorse's head and then went over to congratulate Crispin.

"Great race Crispin, well-deserved win, you're the new champion!"

Everyone watched with pleasure as Crispin was handed the large Crustacean Derby Cup by the mayor, Grandpa Terence. Calvin, Christopher and Chico stood together applauding Crispin.

Calvin then turned to Chico and said, "You see my friend, there was no need to cheat, and your brother won that race fair and square through his own efforts."

"So what have you learned from today's experience, Chico?" Calvin went on to ask.

His friend replied, "Always play fair and square and never CHEAT!"

FRIENDS FOREVER

It was a typical day on the Great Barrier Reef, and all its inhabitants were going about their usual business. At the Sponge Coral School, it was morning breaktime, and all the children were on the playground having fun.

Peter, the parrotfish, was looking for his best friend Patrick, also a parrotfish, but couldn't see him anywhere. Suddenly, as Peter swam near the caretaker's tool shed, he heard a whisper, "Peter, come here, it's me."

"Where are you?" asked Peter. "I can't see you."

"I'm here, behind the tool shed," replied Patrick.

Peter swam behind the shed to find his friend. "What are you doing here, you know it's forbidden to go outside the school fence."

"I know," said Patrick, "but I have to show you this, I've found a monster!"

"Don't be so silly," replied Peter nervously, "there's no such thing."

"Well I've seen one, come behind this rock, and I'll show you!"

"Aaaaaagh!" squealed Peter, as Patrick's fin clamped across his mouth.

"Quiet, silly," commanded Patrick, "It will hear us!"

"What is it?" said Peter. "It's so horrible; it must be about two metres long, and it's got two tails!"

"What do you think that strange lump on its back is for?" asked Peter.

"I don't know," replied his friend, "but look, it's looking this way, I can see two eyes, but its face is covered in glass!"

As the friends stared in amazement at the monster, a voice from behind suddenly disturbed them. "What are you two doing, you know you shouldn't be here, I'm going to tell Miss Mud Crab!"

Patrick and Peter turned to see Daisy, a damselfish, staring at them. Daisy loved to tell tales on her friends, which isn't a very nice thing to do, is it, children?

Peter and Patrick pleaded with Daisy not to tell Miss Mud Crab what they had done, but Daisy just ignored them and swam away, back towards the playground, to report her discovery to Miss Mud Crab.

As Patrick and Peter also made their way back to the playground, they knew they were going to be in trouble with Miss Mud Crab and felt very miserable.

"Line up please children, quietly now and make your way back to the classroom." The children sat at their desks and waited for Miss Mud Crab to begin the next lesson.

"Before we do our story writing, I have something to say to you," said Miss Mud Crab. "Patrick and Peter, would you please tell me why you were outside the school fence when you know it isn't allowed?"

"We're very sorry Miss Mud Crab," replied Patrick, "but we saw a monster and couldn't help looking at it."

"That, Patrick, is a ridiculous excuse for breaking a school rule; I'm sure you saw no such thing!"

"But it's true Miss Mud Crab," said Peter, "I saw it too, it's big and black and has a glass face and two tails!"

To the children's surprise, Miss Mud Crab started to laugh. "Oh, dearie me," she said, "I think I had better go and have a look at this 'monster' myself. You will all sit here in silence until I return, I shall be very quick."

"Shall I come with you, Miss Mud Crab?" asked Patrick, "it might be dangerous."

"No, thank you, Patrick, I will be all right," replied Miss Mud Crab, trying to hide the fact that she seemed to find the whole story very amusing.

Miss Mud Crab was indeed speedy, and as she took her place at the front of the class, the children all felt very relieved that she had returned safely.

"Now, first things first," said Miss Mud Crab. "Patrick and Peter, as you chose to disobey a school rule, you will both stay in the classroom at lunchtime today and write out fifty times, *I must obey the rules, they are there for my safety.*"

"Yes, Miss Mud Crab," Patrick and Peter, replied solemnly.

"As for you Daisy," continued Miss Mud Crab, "I understand that Patrick and Peter may have been in danger because they disobeyed my rules, but I don't believe that was your reason for telling me where they were. I just think, Daisy, that you wanted to get the boys into trouble, and as I don't like the way you seem to love telling tales, you will also receive a punishment. You will also write fifty lines, but yours are to say, *I must not tell tales, it is very unkind*."

"That's not fair," protested Daisy.

"Fair or not, that is what you will do," commanded Miss Mud Crab.

"Now, children, I have decided that instead of story writing today, I will talk to you about this monster, which in fact it is not."

"You will remember the lesson we had when I spoke to you about people, what can anyone tell me about them?"

Gabrielle, the gobyfish, raised her fin and said, "I know Miss Mud Crab, they are creatures that live on the land above the ocean. They can't live like us under the water, because they have to breathe something called oxygen, from the air."

"Excellent, Gabrielle," said Miss Mud Crab, "anyone else?"

Susanna, the surgeonfish, raised her fin and said, "they don't have tails, they walk upright on two things called legs, and they don't have fins like us, they have two arms."

"Super," replied Miss Mud Crab. "Now children, what Patrick and Peter saw was not a monster, but one of these people called a diver. The 'two tails' you thought you saw were, in fact, the diver's legs and the glass across his face is called a mask."

"But I thought people couldn't be under the water like us?" questioned Daisy.

"Well, it's rather clever what they do," continued Miss Mud Crab. "A diver covers himself in something called a wetsuit, which helps to keep his body warm. He wears a mask so that he can see underwater."

"But what was that large lump on his back for?" asked Patrick.

"That is an oxygen cylinder," replied Miss Mud Crab. "It contains the oxygen the diver needs to breathe and a tube from the cylinder, going into his mouth makes this possible, allowing the diver to swim under the water just like we do."

"What were those strange things on the end of his legs, though?" asked Peter.

"They are called fins, just like ours. As the diver moves his feet, they help him to go through the water."

The children were fascinated by what Miss Mud Crab was telling them.

"That is so smart," said Cody the clownfish. "Miss Mud Crab, is there a special suit that we could wear so that we could walk on land like the diver?"

Miss Mud Crab smiled as she replied, "Unfortunately not Cody, but I think we are all thrilled living on this beautiful reef, don't you children?"

"Oh yes," the children replied together.

"But what is the diver doing here?" asked Bella, the butterflyfish?

"That is an excellent question, but one that I will answer after lunch," said Miss Mud Crab. "Now, Patrick,

Peter and Daisy, after you have eaten your meal, come straight back here to do your punishment."

"Yes, Miss Mud Crab," they replied together, but the three young fish now didn't mind writing lines at all, because their naughtiness had led to them hearing the fascinating story of the people who swim under the water.

This still does not mean that they should have disobeyed Miss Mud Crab though does it, children?

After the lunch break, the young fish couldn't wait to hear more about the diver. "Now children, sometimes people dive under the ocean purely for pleasure. They come to look at and admire our beautiful home and also to study the creatures who live here, just like you learn about them."

"However," continued Miss Mud Crab, "I watched the diver that Patrick and Peter saw, and he is in fact here for another reason. You will recall in your last geography lesson, that I explained how some of our coral homes are in danger of being damaged by the hot sun. Some of these very kind people do research and help to rebuild our homes for us, and this is what this diver was doing."

"Wow!" exclaimed Clemmie, Cody's sister, "that is so generous of them, but why would they do this for us, Miss Mud Crab?"

"Because Clemmie, they care about nature, all the animals, birds and sea creatures and where they all live, we are indeed very grateful to them."

The children went home from school that day, feeling very excited about what they had learned and the following morning everyone arrived at school early as they all wanted to catch a glimpse of their diver friend.

When the fish children went out to play at breaktime, they were thrilled to see that their diver friend was working on the coral wall which ran along the edge of the playground and they all watched him in fascination as he went about his work.

Suddenly, the diver, aware that he was being watched, looked up and waved at the fish children. He then produced a small whiteboard, which is like the blackboard you have at school, but which can be used underwater.

The diver then wrote a message on his board, "Hello, little friends, how are you today?"

Miss Mud Crab smiled at the diver and wrote a message of reply on the classroom whiteboard, "We are all very well thank you and very grateful for your help."

"My pleasure," wrote the diver in reply.

During the next few days, the children continued to watch the diver at work during their playtime, and he would always give them a wave.

On the third day, Patrick, feeling comfortable now in the diver's presence, swam right up to his mask and peered through the glass.

"Hello little fellow, what's your name?" wrote the diver.

Patrick took the chalk the diver offered him, and on the diver's board, he wrote, "My name is Patrick, and I was the first to see you, but I thought you were a monster!"

"Well, now you know I'm not, I'm your friend, come to help you," wrote the diver. He erased the message and then wrote, "My name is Danny, and I'm very pleased to meet you, Patrick."

A couple of days later, when Patrick went to say hello to Danny, Danny wrote him another message, "Tomorrow is my last day here, my work is nearly finished."

Patrick felt very sad that he wouldn't be seeing his new friend again, but as Miss Mud Crab had explained, Danny would be moving on to other reefs to continue his work there.

Patrick came up with an idea and went to ask Miss Mud Crab's permission for what he wanted to do. Miss Mud Crab thought Patrick's idea was lovely and told him to go ahead with his plan.

The next day all of the fish children gathered in the playground, to say goodbye to Danny. They all felt so sad but knew his help was needed elsewhere, so it would be very selfish to wish him to stay.

As Danny waved goodbye to his new friends, Miss Mud Crab wrote a message on the whiteboard. "Thank you so much, Danny, for everything you and your friends do for us. We will always remember you and would like to give you a small gift to show our appreciation."

Patrick and Peter then swam towards Danny, carrying a beautiful heart-shaped shell together, which they then handed to Danny.

"Please open the shell," wrote Miss Mud Crab.

As Danny did so, Patrick, who was looking through Danny's mask, saw him gasp in amazement. After a few seconds of staring at the exquisite white pearl that was inside the shell, Danny wrote on his board, "I can't possibly accept this, it is far too generous and belongs to all of you."

As Patrick frantically nodded his head to try and persuade Danny to accept their gift, Miss Mud Crab wrote, "Please take this gift to remember us by; we are so grateful to you for the work you do, and it is our pleasure to give you this pearl."

"In that case, I accept it very gratefully and will think of you all every time I look at it," wrote Danny.

"Come along now children; it's time to get ready to go home, goodbye Danny and thank you again."

"Goodbye Danny," chorused the children as they made their way back inside.

"You may take a moment to say a special goodbye, Patrick," smiled Miss Mud Crab.

As Patrick was left alone with Danny, a small tear trickled down his face. Danny held out his hand and allowed Patrick to swim into it. He showed Patrick the final message he had written, which said, "Please don't be sad Patrick, we should be happy that we have been able to know each other. I want you to take my whiteboard for yourself, and when you are writing on it, you will remember me just as I will remember you."

He continued, "Danny and Patrick, friends forever."

As Patrick gratefully took his gift from Danny, he then planted a goodbye kiss on Danny's mask.

As Patrick entered the classroom, he turned for a final wave to Danny. He couldn't wait for tomorrow's lessons when he could use his new, very precious board.

As Patrick watched Danny swim away, he remembered Danny's parting words, "DANNY AND PATRICK FRIENDS FOREVER."

So you see children, from this story, we learn that it is very important to look after and care for all the earth's creatures and their homes.

You should also remember, that rules are there to protect you and SHOULD NOT BE BROKEN!

Hope to see you again soon, when we next visit our friends on the Reef.

THE MISSING SHELL

One day, Cody, the clownfish and his sister Clemmie, were playing with their friends Billy and Bella, who were butterflyfish. Clown fish, also called anemonefish are very brightly coloured, usually orange or yellow, with white bands or patches on their bodies. The butterflyfish are also very brightly coloured, usually orange, yellow, red, black, silver or white, with different patterns and spots on their bodies. Cody and Clemmie are both orange clownfish with white bands on their bodies, while Bella and Billie, our butterflyfish, are black with silver stripes across them.

The friends were having a lovely time playing chase amongst the coral when Clemmie suggested, "Let's play pass the shell".

"Oh, yes!" the others replied excitedly, and they set about looking for a small, round shell, that they could throw to each other with their noses.

"I've found one!" squealed Bella and so Billy and Cody placed a long piece of seaweed on the ocean floor, to act as a net. They took their positions on one side of it, while Clemmie and Bella went to the other side of the net.

What a lovely time they had, trying to push the shell over the net and back again, just like you might play a game of tennis.

Suddenly, their game was interrupted by the sound of laughter, and as they turned to see who was there, poor Cody dropped the shell they were playing with. They saw the lionfish gang, watching them and laughing.

The lionfish is a quite beautiful and fascinating-looking fish. It is usually white, with reddish brown stripes and long, fan-like fins. Although very attractive to look at, the lionfish is very dangerous.

The two lionfish brothers, Lenny and Lawrence and their two friends, Lance and Lionel, were being very unkind and made fun of Cody and his friends. "Clumsy Cody," sang Lenny, "can't catch the shell."

"Cody's a clown, a clumsy, silly clown," chanted Lawrence. Then they all joined in together. "Cody's a clown, a clumsy, silly clown."

"Leave Cody alone!" shouted Clemmie.

"Don't be so unkind," said Bella.

"Go away and leave us alone, you're just a lot of

bullies!" shouted Billie.

But the lionfish gang didn't stop teasing Cody; they just kept singing, "Cody's a cissy, Cody's a Cissy."

Suddenly, Cody turned and swam away, looking very sad and hurt. "Come on," said Clemmie, to Bella and Billie, "let's follow Cody, we don't want to stay and argue with these horrible, mean lionfish, Cody needs us."

After a short while, the three friends found Cody hiding behind a large crop of coral and they could see that he was crying. "Please don't cry, Cody," said Clemmie, feeling very sorry for her brother.

"They're just not worth crying over," comforted Billie.

"But they're right," sobbed Cody. "Look at me, I do look like a clown, and after all, my family are called clown fish!"

"Yes," replied Bella, "but that's only a kind of nickname, your colours are so vivid and bright, and as you know, your real name is anemonefish, and I think that sounds really beautiful, don't you Billie?"

"I sure do," replied Billie. "What we need to do is come up with an idea that will show those bullies how clever you are Cody, we must all put our thinking caps on."

"Thanks, guys," said Cody, "but I don't hold out much hope. We had better be getting home now, or Mum and Dad will start to worry." With that, the friends said goodbye to one other and made their way home.

The next morning, Cody and Clemmie went out again, to play with Billie and Bella. Cody was feeling better today, but so far none of the friends had come up with a plan to foil the lionfish bullies.

"What shall we play?" asked Bella,

"Hide and seek!" squealed Clemmie. "I'll cover my eyes and count first, and you all go and hide."

Just as the friends were about to swim off, Cody said, "Hold on guys, what's that noise?" They all listened, and it soon became apparent that the sound was laughter, "It's those horrible lionfish, up to their tricks again" said Cody. "I wonder who they're teasing now."

"Come on," replied Billie. "Let's go and see, maybe we can help."

The friends made their way to where the sound of laughter was coming from, and it gradually became louder and louder. As they turned a coral corner, they saw that it was indeed the lionfish gang, and they were laughing at their friend Debbie. Debbie was a tiny, beautiful, bright blue damselfish and she was crying and shouting at the bullies, "Let me have it back, it's mine!"

As Bella put her fin around Debbie to comfort her, Cody asked what the lionfish had taken.

"I found the most beautiful shell," sobbed Debbie

"Now try and calm down and tell us what has happened," said Billie.

Debbie took some deep breaths and told her friends about the shell she had found. She was going to make it into a necklace for her mummy's birthday, but the lionfish had taken it from her and thrown it into the anemone coral, which is very poisonous, so she couldn't go in and get it back.

"Ha, ha, ha," laughed the bullies. "Ask cowardly

Cody to get it back for you," taunted Lance.

"Don't be so silly," cried Debbie. "You know that fish can't go into the coral, it is poisonous."

"We dare you, Cody, go in and get the shell, or are you too scared?" said Lawrence. The lionfish then started singing, "Scaredy scared Cody."

As the lionfish continued teasing Cody, Billie swam over and whispered in his ear. "You know what Cody, this is your perfect chance to teach those bullies a lesson. We are aware you are the only fish who can go into the anemone coral safely, as it is your home, but the bullies don't know that do they?"

"Wow," replied Cody. "That's such a smart plan Billie, watch this!" Cody then swam right up close to Lenny and looked him straight in the eyes. "If I go into that coral and find Debbie's shell, will you promise to change your ways and stop being so unkind to everyone?"

"That is such a ridiculous suggestion," said Lenny, "Of course we will agree because we know you won't do it!"

"Oh, yes, I will," said Cody, "but before I do, you

64

have to promise that you will change."

"Humour him," said Lawrence. "He'll never go in there."

"Okay, Cody, we make the promise of the lionfish gang, if you succeed, we will be good."

"Don't do it, Cody!" screamed Debbie, but Clemmie whispered in her ear that it was safe for Cody to go into the coral, so she shouldn't worry.

With that, Cody turned and started swimming towards the coral, and suddenly Lennie cried, "Gosh, he's going to do it, I thought he was joking, stop, Cody, STOP!"

But Cody didn't stop; he swam into the coral, and as the lionfish started arguing in fear and blaming one another for goading Cody into doing this hazardous thing, Cody's friends just watched calmly, enjoying the bullies' discomfort.

After a few minutes, Cody reappeared, proudly waving Debbie's beautiful shell. His friends cheered loudly as the bullies' jaws dropped open in complete amazement.

"How on earth did you do that Cody?" asked Lionel.

"You are so brave, we will never call you a coward again," said Lance.

"Just make sure you keep your promise," replied Cody. "Why would you want to be so mean anyway?"

"You have so many friends, and we don't have any," said Lenny. "I guess we're just jealous."

"But if you were kind and helpful, instead of mean and nasty, all the other fish would be your friends too," said Clemmie.

"Do you think so?" asked Lawrence.

"I know so," replied Cody, "and let's start with you all being friends with Bella, Billie, Clemmie, Debbie and me, but you have to agree to accept our motto."

"Of course, we will!" the lionfish all shouted together. "What is the motto?"

Cody replied, "Kind and helpful is our way, to play together every day, all for one and one for all, the ocean's creatures big and small." So they all linked fins in a large circle and sang the motto together, maybe you would like to join in, too?

"Kind and helpful is our way,
to play together every day,
all for one and one for all,
the ocean's creatures big and small".

"Hooray," they all cheered and from that day onwards the lionfish gang never bullied or teased again.

So you see children, what our fish friends have taught us, is that you should always do your best to be kind and helpful to everyone, no matter who they are or if they are different to you. You wouldn't like to be bullied, would you? Be sure you never bully anyone at all, be kind and helpful, and you too will make lots and lots of friends.

LUCY'S LUCKY ESCAPE

This story is about a lemonpeel angelfish called Lucy. She is small and is a lovely bright yellow colour and is beautiful. One day, Lucy was swimming backwards and forwards outside her reef home, feeling very lonely and fed up.

All of Lucy's friends were busy doing other things today, and so she had nobody to play with. Lucy's Mummy Lilian came out to look for her and asked her why she was looking so sad. "I don't know what to do," replied Lucy, "My friends are all busy today, and I have nobody to play with."

"Well", said Lilian, "that's no reason to be so downhearted, why don't you come and help me clean the house, we can enjoy working together."

"I don't want to do that, it's just boring!" shouted Lucy very rudely.

"Please don't speak to me in that way, Lucy," said her mummy. "It is very rude and unacceptable. Now, you will go and tidy your room at once; it certainly needs doing!"

With that, Lilian went back into the house, and Lucy was about to follow her, very sulkily, when suddenly a voice said, "Hello, young lady, why are you looking so miserable?"

Lucy turned and saw a large, honeycomb moray eel, looking at her. Moray eels look like snakes, but they aren't, they are fish and can grow to 300 centimetres in length. The honeycomb moray is also called the leopard moray because its skin looks like the skin of a leopard.

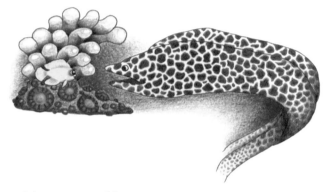

"Are you speaking to me?" asked Lucy.

"Yes, I am," replied the eel.

"Oh, well," continued Lucy, feeling pleased that somebody was at least taking some notice of her, "I'm fed up because I have no friends to play with today, and my mummy said I have to tidy my room. I don't want to do that; it's too boring."

"I agree with you," said the eel. "Sounds very annoying to me too; I'm going on an adventure today, much more fun."

"You are so lucky, I wish I could go on an adventure," said Lucy.

"Well, why don't you come with me?" asked the eel. "My name is Maurice, and I would enjoy your company."

"Are you sure?" said Lucy excitedly. " My name is

Lucy, and I would love to come with you, but how long will it take?"

"Not too long, you still have time to tidy your room later," replied Maurice.

"Thank you so much, I will come with you, but I must just tell Mummy where I'm going," said Lucy.

"No time for that, we must get going," said Maurice. "Anyway, your mummy probably wouldn't let you come with me on my adventure, so if you don't tell her, she can't stop you, can she?"

Lucy knew that this was the wrong thing to do, her mummy and daddy had always taught her never to talk to or go off with strange fish because it was very dangerous to do so. However, Lucy so wanted to go with the eel on his adventure, that she ignored what her parents had said and decided to go. Lucy was certainly very naughty and very silly, wasn't she children?

"Okay, let's go," said Lucy and as Maurice set off, she followed him, not giving any thought to the possible dangers she may be about to face.

They swam for a long time, and Lucy began to feel frustrated. "When is our adventure going to start," she asked. "This is just swimming, I could have done that by myself."

"Almost there, just a couple more minutes," replied Maurice. No sooner had he spoken than Lucy saw a large dark object, looming up in front of them. As they swam nearer, she began to feel a little nervous. "Where are we?" she asked, "I don't think I like it here."

"This is a shipwreck," Maurice explained. "It's the

remains of a ship that has sunk beneath the waves, and this is where my friends and I are going to have a party."

"Am I coming to the party too?" asked Lucy, excitedly.

"Oh yes, you will be there, ha, ha, ha!" laughed Maurice.

"Why are you laughing at me?" asked Lucy, suddenly wishing that she hadn't disobeyed her mummy and had never followed the eel to this dark, frightening place.

"Because my sweet, silly little Lucy, you are certainly going to be at the party, but not to join in the fun. You are going to be part of our feast; I'm sure you will taste delicious!"

"NO, no!" screamed Lucy. "I don't want to stay here, you tricked me, I just want to go home!"

"Save your tears, no one will hear you," said Maurice as suddenly more eels started to appear from the wreck.

Lucy was shaking with fear as the eels began to close

in around her. There was no escape for her, as they forced her into a piece of net that was hanging from the wreck. "See you later," scoffed Maurice, "we're off to find more food for our feast."

Lucy was suddenly left alone, trapped and very frightened, she started to cry. She tried to wriggle free but the more she tried, the tighter the net seemed to wrap around her.

After a while, Lucy realised that there was no escape for her and stopped struggling, "Why, oh, why, hadn't I listened to my parents?" she thought. "Mummy, Daddy, please come and save me!" screamed Lucy, but she knew they wouldn't come because they didn't have any idea where she was.

"I know I've been very disobedient and stupid," sobbed Lucy, "but I'm sorry, and I don't want to be eaten!"

Suddenly, Lucy was taken by surprise, as the sand on the ocean bed, near to the wreck, started to move. "What's happening now?" thought Lucy. She began to shake and cry again in fear. Then, before her eyes, rising from the seabed, she saw a huge, wonderful manta ray.

Manta Rays are fish, which have a flat body and can be oval or triangular in shape and can grow to over 4 metres. They are usually black on top and white underneath, and they have very powerful pectoral fins, which look like wings, which help them to swim and glide through the water.

The manta ray that appeared before Lucy was huge, and as she stared in amazement, Lucy seemed to recognise the markings on its back. "Oh, my, goodness" cried Lucy, "Mr Martin, is that you? Help me, help PLEASE," she shouted. "I'm here, up here, HELP ME!"

Suddenly, the manta ray turned and saw Lucy. It was indeed Mr Martin, and Lucy knew him because he was a friend of her father's. "Is that you young Lucy?" he asked. "What on earth are you doing trapped in there?"

"I followed Maurice, the moray eel because he promised me an adventure, but he lied, they are going to eat me and…"

Lucy starting crying again and Martin said, "I think someone has been a very naughty and silly little fish, but the important thing right now is to get you away from here before the eels return."

"Oh, yes, please," sobbed Lucy. "Please, Mr Martin, just take me back home."

In no time at all Martin had released Lucy and with

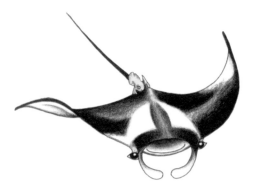

her safely on his large back, set off to return her to her home on Red Coral Drive. As they arrived at Lucy's home, her mummy and daddy came rushing out, looking very, very worried. "Lucy, where on earth have you been?" cried her mummy.

"We were so worried about you. You know you must never go off without telling us," said Daddy. "Anything could have happened!"

"I think that explanations and punishment can wait," said Mummy, "all Lucy needs now is a great big hug from us both."

"We can't thank you enough, Martin, for rescuing our Lucy," said Daddy.

"Please bring your wife for dinner on Saturday," added Mummy.

"Thank you, that would be lovely, I'll see you then," said Martin and off he went, home to his family.

As Lucy felt her parent's fins fold around her in a loving hug, she realised that they cared about her so much, even when they were cross with her, and she vowed that she would never again disobey her parents, because they did know best.

Lucy was fortunate wasn't she children, to have been rescued from those nasty eels? If Mr Martin hadn't been there, this story would have a very different, unhappy ending.

The lesson we learn from this story is that you should never speak to strangers or go anywhere with them, without telling your mummy or daddy first.

Even if they offer you sweets or promise something nice, you must always say NO. Always remember these rules and always listen to what your mummy or daddy tell you and then you will stay safe and happy.

SUSIE STARTS SCHOOL

It was Monday morning, and there was much activity on the Reef. It was the first day of the new school term and all the fish children wanted to arrive on time. Some of the children were moving on to new schools and so they were feeling very excited, but also a little nervous.

Two of these small fish were best friends, Susie and Sally Shrimp. They were both starting at junior school and were going along together.

"Come along Susie," called Mrs Shrimpson, Susie's mother, "your breakfast is ready, and Sally will be here shortly."

"Coming Mummy," replied Susie. "I am just putting my new colouring pencils into my satchel."

No sooner had Susie finished her breakfast when there was a knock at the door. "That will be Sally, I'll go, Mummy," said Susie excitedly.

"Hi, Susie, hello, Mrs Shrimpson," said Sally. "Daddy asked me to say good morning, but he was running late for work, so he left me here and went straight off. Are you ready to go Susie?"

"Yes, all set," replied her friend.

"Right," said Susie's mother, "straight to school now and I will watch from outside the house to see you go to school safely. Have a good day girls, see you later."

The girls set off and soon reached the school, which was on the same street as Susie's house. Before going through the gate, they turned and waved to Mrs Shrimpson.

Suddenly, both children felt very nervous, not quite sure what to do next. Their nerves soon disappeared though as a young teacher approached them and smiled warmly. Susie and Sally recognised Miss Denise, from their previous visit to their new school, when they had spent a whole day there to meet their teacher and learn their way around.

"Good morning girls," said Miss Denise brightly, "please join the group of children waiting on the steps, we will be going in shortly, when everyone is here."

The children liked Miss Denise instantly; she was a young, pretty dolphin and always seemed to be smiling.

The children went to join the group and immediately felt at ease when they saw some of their friends from infant school, who were going to be in their new class. They saw Clemmie the clownfish and Bella the butterflyfish. Clemmie and Bella's brothers, Cody and Billie were to be in a different class.

They also saw Daisy and Debbie the damselfish and Lucy, the angelfish.

"Hi, everyone," said Susie, and all the children, excitedly, started talking until they were interrupted by Miss Denise's voice.

"Quiet please everyone, you will remember from your visit that you each have a named peg in the cloakroom. I would like you to please hang your coats on your pegs, put your lunchboxes on the table and then come into the classroom and choose yourselves a seat."

A few minutes later, everyone was sitting down in their new classroom, waiting to discover what their first lesson was to be.

"Now," began Miss Denise, "I thought we would start today, by decorating our classroom, to make it a fascinating and pleasant place to be. Our theme is going to be about nature, and I have lots of stencils here, which you can choose from to make your nature pictures. There are many different creatures, not only from the ocean but also land animals. Wild animals such as lions, tigers and bears and tame animals such as cats, dogs and rabbits, which some people have as pets."

Miss Denise smiled at the children and continued speaking. "If you prefer, your picture can be of trees and plants, flowers and coral. When you have made your decision, please come quietly and select your stencils, there are plenty for everyone."

The children looked on excitedly as Miss Denise pointed towards lots of materials they could use. "You will find pencils, colouring pencils if you need them and paints, already on your tables, so get started everyone and have fun!"

Halfway through the morning, the children went out into the playground and played toss the shell, chase and seaweed skipping.

They then spent the rest of the morning finishing their nature pictures and helping Miss Denise to hang them on the classroom walls.

"What a fantastic job you have done, children!" exclaimed Miss Denise. "We are now surrounded by the wonders of nature, and during your nature study lessons, we shall learn about many of these fascinating creatures, objects and places. Now children, please go and wash your hands, collect your lunchboxes and make your way to the school hall for lunch."

As the children began to leave their classroom, Miss Denise called after Susie. "Susie, before you go, would you please put one of these writing books at everyone's place for me?"

"Of course, Miss Denise," replied Susie, "I'll see you in the hall shortly," she said to Sally.

However, when she entered the hall, Sally was nowhere to be seen. Susie asked if anyone had seen her and Daisy said that she last saw her in the cloakroom.

Susie made her way to the cloakroom and as she entered, she heard the sound of someone crying. "Is that you Sally?" she asked in a very concerned voice.

"I'm over here," replied her friend.

"Whatever is the matter?" asked Susie, putting one of her long legs around her friend's shoulders to comfort her; shrimps don't have arms, just lots of legs.

"Two of the year nine children, have taken my lunch," sobbed Sally.

"What, why?" questioned Susie. "Now, dry your tears and tell me what has happened."

Once Sally had calmed down, she explained to Susie that Leticia and Lydia, the lionfish, had said she had to give them her lunch. If she refused, Leticia wouldn't choose Samantha, Sally's sister to be in the School Competitive Swimming Team, of which Leticia was captain.

"That's so unfair," said Susie, "not only to threaten you like that, but to use Samantha as their secret weapon. When the teachers know about this, I'm sure Leticia won't be captain of swimming any more."

"No, Susie, you mustn't tell anyone!" exclaimed Sally.

"You have to tell, they are nasty bullies and can't be allowed to get away with this," replied Susie.

"Lydia said that if I tell, they will still find a way to stop Samantha going to the swimming trials, I have to keep quiet for my sister's sake."

"This is ridiculous, there must be something we can do," replied Susie angrily.

As Sally started to cry again, Susie said, "I know; we could put lots of sea pepper in your sandwiches, and they definitely won't come back for more!"

80

This made Sally smile, but not for long. "It won't work Susie, they will be even angrier, and Samantha will suffer."

"Right," said Susie, "we have to think of a plan to stop this, but meanwhile you will share my lunch, there's plenty for both of us."

"Thank you, Susie, you're such a good friend."

After lunch and outside play, the children started to write a story in their new writing books about what they had done during the school holidays. The afternoon finished with Miss Denise reading them a lovely story about a human girl called Cinderella, who was bullied and made to work all the time by her two mean stepsisters. In the end, though, right wins through, a prince rescues Cinderella, and they live happily ever after. I expect children that some of you know this story too.

That evening at home, Susie tried desperately to come up with a plan to stop Sally being bullied. Susie knew that bullying was always wrong and that you should always tell your parents or teacher if you are, or know of someone who is being bullied. She knew that she should tell her parents or Miss Denise what was happening, but she had promised Sally she wouldn't, and it was also wrong to break a promise. What was she to do to help her friend?

The next morning, Susie asked her mummy to pack her some extra lunch as she found she was starving the day before. Mrs Shrimpson did this feeling pleased that Susie must be working well at school to give her an enormous appetite.

This continued for a whole week, Susie sharing her extra lunch with Sally, while Sally continued to give hers to Leticia and Lydia. She couldn't ask her mother for more food because Leticia and Lydia would just take that too.

"Once the trials are over, and Samantha has hopefully made the team, I'm sure this will all stop," Sally said one lunchtime.

"The trials aren't for another three weeks," replied Susie. "Putting that aside, Leticia may deliberately not select Samantha, and all of this will have been for nothing."

"Please don't be cross with me, Susie, I just don't know what else to do," continued Sally.

"I'm not cross, well not with you," replied Susie. "I just wish we could find a solution to our problem."

By the time Susie arrived home that afternoon, she knew what she had to do. After dinner, she asked her mummy and daddy if she could talk to them about something significant.

They sat down together, and Susie began, "If you make a promise to a friend is it ever all right to break that promise?" she asked her parents.

"Well Susie, you should always try to keep your promises, but sometimes it turns out that it just isn't possible," said mummy.

"Also, if you, keeping a promise, means that somebody may get hurt in any way, then I feel you must break it and confide in someone who can help you. If ever you are in that situation, Susie," continued her mummy, "you know you can always speak to Daddy and me about anything."

Susie took a deep breath and told her parents everything that had been going on at school with Sally and the bullies. When she had finished speaking, her daddy said, "That was very brave of you to tell us what has been happening Susie, it was the right thing to do because now we will speak to Sally's parents and they will be able to go to the school and sort the problem out. Mummy and I are very proud of you, but if anything like this ever happens again, you must tell us straight away."

"I will Daddy," replied Susie, "but I feel so sorry because I have broken my promise to Sally and she might not want to be my friend any more."

"That would be very sad if it happens," said mummy. "However, you have still done the right thing, Susie. Although Sally might be a little cross with you for a while, I think she will be grateful to you for bringing this problem to an end and I'm sure will forgive you for breaking your promise."

" At least I can now go back to making you a standard size lunch again!" said Mummy. Everyone laughed, as Susie felt very relieved to know that her parents would now make sure the bullying stopped.

After Mr and Mrs Shrimpson had spoken to them, Mr and Mrs Shrimp-Smith, Sally's parents, immediately went to the school and told Mr Stewart, the Stingray headteacher, and Miss Denise about the bullying.

Leticia, Lydia and their parents were summoned to Mr Stewart's office, and on hearing what their children had done, Leticia and Lydia's parents were horrified and very cross.

"Don't I pack you enough lunch?" questioned Mrs Lionson.

"Yes, you do Mummy," replied Leticia solemnly. "It just started as a joke and then when we realised that Sally would do anything to give her sister a chance to be in the School Swimming Team, we carried on because it felt good to be in control."

"Felt good? FELT GOOD!" exclaimed Mr Stewart. "I'll tell you what will feel good, young lady, your punishments!"

"What do you have to say for yourselves?" asked Miss Denise. "Would you like to be treated the way you treated Sally?"

"N… no," replied Lydia and started to cry. "I am sorry Mr Stewart, it was cruel and stupid, and I promise not to misbehave again."

"Save your tears, Lydia," said Mr Stewart. "They are tears of shame, but make no difference to how I feel about your behaviour. What do you have to say, Leticia?" Mr Stewart continued.

"I agree with Lydia completely, and I admit it was my idea, not hers, she just went along with me. I too am very sorry and will never behave like that again."

"Very well," said Mr Stewart, "I am sure your parents will have plenty to say to you later," and even as he spoke, the girls' parents nodded in agreement, all looking very, very cross with their daughters.

Mr Stewart continued speaking. "You will both begin by sincerely apologising to Sally and her friend Susie, who was brave enough to say what was happening. That is a real friendship, and you can both learn a valuable lesson from that. You will both write a letter of apology to Mr and Mrs Shrimpson for the appalling way you treated their daughter, and you will both do two weeks' detention after school each day. The first week will be spent writing lines about the wrongs and effects of bullying and your second week will be spent weeding the school nature garden. Hopefully, after that, you will have learned your lesson. I'm sure this will come as no surprise Leticia, but you will of course no longer captain the School Swimming Team. I think perhaps Samantha Shrimp-Smith would be a good candidate to take your place? You may think my punishments harsh, but I will never tolerate bullying in this school, and if ever you behave in such a fashion again, I will not hesitate to suspend you from school."

With that, Mr Stewart turned to Miss Denise. "Now, would you please go and fetch Sally and Susie Miss Denise?"

"Of course, Headmaster," replied Miss Denise.

Five minutes later Sally and Susie had joined the others in Mr Stewart's office. "Leticia and Lydia have something they wish to say," said Mr Stewart.

"We are very sorry for stealing your lunch and bullying you Sally, it was very unkind and wrong of us," said Leticia.

"We hope that you may be able to forgive us, Sally, we will never treat anyone like that again."

"Thank you for your apology, and as long as you have learnt your lesson, we will say no more about it," replied Sally.

Mr Lionson, Leticia's father, then said, "I would also like to apologise on behalf of my wife and Mr and Mrs Lion-Jones, for our children's dreadful behaviour, they certainly haven't heard the last of it from us, I can assure you."

"Thank you all," replied Sally. "But please don't be too hard on Leticia and Lydia. We all make mistakes, but as long as we learn from them, that is what matters, and I believe that they have learnt from theirs."

As Leticia, Lydia and their parents then left the office, Susie turned to Sally and said, "I'm so sorry to have broken my promise Sally, but it was the right thing to do, I hope you can forgive me too."

Sally put her legs around her friend and hugged her warmly. "There is nothing to forgive you for, you are a lovely friend, and I'm very grateful to you."

"Right girls, I think you had better return to class now, and Miss Denise would you please ask Samantha Shrimp-Smith to come and see me?"

Mr Stewart noticed the worried look on Sally's face and said, "Don't look so worried Sally, Samantha isn't in any trouble, I just want to tell her that she automatically qualifies for a place on the School Swimming Team, as its new captain!"

"That's wonderful!" squealed Sally as she hugged Susie joyfully.

"I'm so happy, Susie," said Sally as they made their way back to their classroom. School is going to be such fun from now on."

"I'm sure it is," replied her friend. "The only thing is, we now have double maths!"

The friends linked legs and laughed together as they joined their friends in their lovely nature-themed classroom and opened their maths books happily.

So you see children, although you have already learnt from the Reef story of *The Missing Shell*, how wrong bullying is, you have now gained something else, from this story.

If ever you are bullied or know of someone who is being bullied, never be afraid to tell your mummy, daddy or your teacher. They will always help, so be brave and SPEAK OUT!

See you again soon, when we share our next Reef Adventure.

THE STOLEN SATCHEL

It was Monday morning on the Reef, and the children were all gathered in the playground, laughing and chatting together, about what they had done at the weekend.

Suddenly, Oswald Octopus came rushing into the playground singing, "Happy birthday to me, happy birthday to me, happy birthday dear Oswald, happy birthday to me! Hi everyone, it's my birthday today, you can all wish me a happy day."

"I think we already know that, Oswald," said Susanna the sturgeonfish, but Happy Birthday anyway."

"Happy birthday," the other children chorused, but somewhat reluctantly. Oswald was a bit of a show-off, and nobody liked the way he behaved.

"Look, everyone, at my fantastic, very expensive new satchel, don't you all wish you had one like it?"

"Stop showing off Oswald," said Patrick, the parrotfish. "It doesn't matter how much a gift costs, it's the thought behind it that matters."

"You're just jealous Patrick because your satchel is old and worn," replied Oswald.

"Don't be so horrid!" said Cody the clownfish. "I wouldn't want your satchel, even if you gave it to me, not if it made me nasty like you."

"I don't care what any of you think," said Oswald, "and I'm not inviting any of you to my party, so there!"

As the children thought that they wouldn't want to go to Oswald's party anyway, the school bell rang, and they all made their way into the classroom.

"Take your seats please everyone," said Miss Denise, "I would like a volunteer to hand out these spelling tests, which you are doing this morning."

"Me Miss Denise," exclaimed Oswald, "it's my birthday, so I should be your helper today."

"Oh... er, very well Oswald and a happy birthday to you," replied Miss Denise.

"Can I show you my new satchel that I had for my birthday, Miss Denise?" asked Oswald.

"Not now Oswald, but you may show me at break time."

Everyone settled down to do the spelling test, trying hard to remember the words they had to learn for weekend homework and following this they had a maths lesson.

The children were all glad when breaktime came, and as they hurried out into the playground, Oswald rushed to the cloakroom to collect his satchel to show Miss Denise.

Suddenly, a loud scream came from the cloakroom, and Miss Denise hurried in to find Oswald screaming in anguish. "It's not here; my lovely new satchel is gone, it's been stolen!"

"Now, now, calm down, Oswald," said Miss Denise, "I'm sure that there is a logical explanation. You can't make accusations like that without any evidence."

"I know the other children took it, they were all so jealous of me, because I have a new, shiny satchel, and they don't!"

"That's enough Oswald; I will not listen to you saying such a dreadful thing. I do not believe the other children are jealous of you, but like me, they do not like the way that you boast all the time. It is very unpleasant and certainly won't help you to make any friends. Now, come along and let's find out what has happened to your satchel."

Miss Denise summoned the children back into the classroom and asked them if anyone knew the whereabouts of Oswald's satchel. Everyone denied any knowledge of how it had disappeared and Miss Denise decided that everyone should join in a search for the satchel.

The children hunted everywhere, in the classrooms, the cloakrooms, the school hall and the dining room. They then went outside and searched the play areas and the nature gardens, but to no avail, Oswald's satchel was nowhere to be seen. Miss Denise had no choice but to report the matter to Mr Stewart the Stingray headmaster, who called a special assembly of the whole school.

"It has been brought to my attention," began Mr Stewart, "that a very serious matter has occurred. A satchel has gone missing from the junior cloakroom and after Miss Denise and her pupils carried out a thorough search of the school, it still hasn't been found. Sadly, this suggests that it may have been stolen. I will not tolerate such behaviour and do not wish to believe that any of you would do such a thing. Therefore, if anyone can throw any light on the satchel's disappearance, I expect them to come to my office before the end of school today. Now, you may all return to your classrooms, and I trust this matter will be resolved very quickly."

By the end of school there were no new developments regarding Oswald's satchel, and therefore Mr Stewart had to discuss the matter with Mr and Mrs Octopus. He promised that he would do everything he could to solve the problem, but Mr and Mrs Octopus were furious and said that if the satchel was not found very soon, then they would take the matter to the Reef Police.

Mr Stewart certainly didn't want this, but as he made his way home that evening, he was struggling to know how to solve the problem and avoid getting the police involved.

The next morning, after registration, Miss Denise instructed her class to go to the cloakroom and change for their PE lesson.

As Billie the butterflyfish passed Oswald on his way to his changing room peg; he noticed that Oswald was struggling to get his PE bag off of his own peg.

"What have you got in there Oswald?" he asked. "The Mer Family Jewels?"

"None of your business," snapped Oswald.

"Come on Oswald, show us what you're hiding," said Daisy the damselfish.

"Come on Oswald, show us, show us," chanted the children.

"It's private, leave me alone," replied Oswald as he began to blush and look embarrassed.

Suddenly, Lennie the lionfish grabbed Oswald's PE bag, and on opening it, he stared in amazement.

"What is it?" asked Cody the clownfish.

"Show us what you've found," said Billie.

"No, no, you can't do this!" cried Oswald in panic.

As Lennie withdrew an object from Oswald's PE bag, all of the children gasped at what he was holding, Oswald's MISSING SATCHEL!

At that point, Miss Denise entered the cloakroom, to see what all the commotion was about.

"Oswald lied Miss Denise," said Lennie, "his satchel wasn't missing at all, he had hidden it in his PE bag."

"Is this right?" asked Miss Denise in amazement. "Why on earth would you do such a thing, trying to point the blame at somebody else for a crime that was never committed?"

Oswald just looked at his feet and didn't answer; he realised he was now in big trouble.

"You children will please go into the hall for your PE lesson, where the teacher is waiting and YOU,Oswald, will come with me immediately to Mr Stewart's office.

On hearing what Miss Denise had to say, Mr Stewart began to question Oswald as to why he committed this terrible deed.

"The other children won't be friends with me, and I wanted to pay them back, so I thought I would get them into trouble by accusing them of stealing my satchel, but of course it was a stupid idea, I see that now."

"It most certainly was," replied Mr Stewart, "not only stupid but unkind, thoughtless and inconsiderate! You gave no thought whatsoever to the time that has been wasted searching for a missing satchel; that wasn't missing at all. Were you going to allow your parents to get the Reef Police involved, knowing that there was no crime to answer for, except for a silly young octopus feeling sorry for himself and having no regard for the trouble he was causing?"

"I d... do not know sir," sobbed Oswald, "I d... didn't mean it to go so far."

"Well, young man, it has indeed gone too far, and now I must call your parents and explain what their son has been up to."

Oswald's parents were extremely cross to discover what Oswald had done, and on hearing Mr Stewart's decision, they could only agree that Oswald deserved his punishment.

"I am very tempted to suspend you, Oswald," began Mr Stewart, "but I don't think that will teach you anything or be of benefit. I think you should face up to the people you have offended and have to deal with their reactions to you. You will stand up in assembly tomorrow morning, in front of the school, confess to what you have done and express your sincere apologies to everyone. You will also do after school detention for two weeks, during which you will do work set for you by Miss Denise."

With that Oswald left with his parents, feeling very sheepish and embarrassed. He also knew that Mr Stewart's punishment wasn't the end of it. He would have to listen to his parent's punishment when they arrived home and even worse, face everyone at school tomorrow.

Oswald wished he had never been so stupid and done what he did.

The next morning, Oswald was shaking in his shoes, (all eight of them!), as he climbed the steps up onto the stage, from where he was to address the school. "I want to say that I was very wrong to try and blame any of you for stealing my satchel. It was never stolen at all; it was just a silly plan I made up, to get back at my classmates because they won't be my friends."

Oswald took a deep breath and continued, "I want to say that I know it was a thoughtless and bad thing to do, and I am truly sorry. I know now that I will never make any friends, but I guess that's the price I have to pay. I understand you will all be very angry with me, but please know that I sincerely regret my actions."

Mr Stewart then stepped forward and told Oswald to join his classmates.

"Before any of you judge Oswald, please bear in mind that it took a lot of courage for him to face you all this morning. What he did was certainly wrong and unacceptable, but please ask yourselves, have you never made a mistake or done something you regret later? Please think on that, now school dismissed."

Everyone returned to class, and Oswald's bad behaviour wasn't discussed further. However, at playtime, he was completely ignored by everyone, they were still angry at his antics.

"He needs to be taught a lesson," said Lawrence the lionfish.

"I agree," said Lennie.

"Hold on a minute, guys," continued Peter, a parrotfish. "Remember what Mr Stewart said. Have you never behaved badly? I recall the reputation the Lionfish Gang once had, did the way you cruelly bullied everyone, make you any better than Oswald?"

"Are you saying his behaviour was okay then?" questioned Gabrielle the gobyfish, as the lionfish looked very sheepish.

"No, not at all," replied Peter, "but I do believe he is truly sorry, and perhaps we should try to find out why he did it."

"Everyone deserves a second chance, don't they?" said Cody.

So the children gathered around Oswald, and as he appeared very nervous, Peter told him, "It's all right Oswald, we're not going to hurt you, we just want to know why you behaved the way you did."

"Oswald began to explain very slowly, " I just want to be friends with you all, but you won't accept me, and I don't know why."

"Well," replied Peter, " I would have thought that was obvious, but I will tell you anyway. You are such a show-off Oswald, and you are always bragging about what you have and what you do. The thing is, we don't like it, and we don't care. We are friends because we care about each other, not about what we have or don't have. That is simply not important."

"Oh, dear," sighed Oswald, "I thought it would impress you, but I seem to have got things completely wrong, I'm so sorry guys."

"Well, I believe that we should make a deal," said Gabrielle. "You Oswald will try your hardest to be far more humble and caring towards others, and in return, we will all be friends with you."

"Does everyone agree with my suggestion?" asked Gabrielle.

"Yes," replied the children in unison.

"I don't know what to say," said Oswald, "I can't believe you would all want to be friends with me after the way I treated you."

"That's what friends do," replied Peter, "they look out for each other."

During lessons that afternoon, Peter and Gabrielle both asked to be excused to use the bathrooms.

"Very well, but hurry back," said Miss Denise.

When they returned, Peter and Gabrielle both had a big smile on their faces. Knowing the reason why, the rest of the children smiled too, all except Oswald.

"What is everyone smiling at?" he asked Peter quietly.

"Don't worry; you'll find out soon enough," replied Peter.

As the children entered the cloakroom at going home time, Oswald let out a cry. "I don't believe it, I know none of you is responsible, but my satchel is missing again!"

The children all started to laugh. "Come with us Oswald; we have something to show you," said Cody. Oswald followed everyone into the playground and following Cody's instructions, looked up to the school roof. What he saw made him smile, and he felt a tear of happiness trickling down his face.

Hanging from the flagpole on the roof was his satchel and along the edge of the roof was a banner, which said, "Everyone deserves a second chance Oswald, but remember, friendship is worth far more than this satchel."

"Thanks, guys, I will be the best friend ever from now on."

"In that case," asked Billie, "when's this party of yours?"

"Saturday at three o'clock," replied Oswald, "of course everyone is invited!"

"Hooray!" cheered the children and they all went home happy that afternoon, looking forward to Saturday's party.

So, children, we learn quite a lot from this story, don't we?

Firstly it is always wrong TO STEAL, never be tempted. Secondly, TELLING LIES is also wrong, always tell the truth, even if you think you may get into trouble for something you have done.

Finally, remember, FRIENDSHIP is one of the most important things in life. Like your friends for who they are and not for what they have.

GOODBYE FOR NOW.